For crazy mixed up folks who still get a kick out
of life and living

Arcobar Yarns

Whimsical Stories with Heart.

Arcobar Yarns: Whimsical Stories with Heart.

© Bala Mudaly 2023
ISBN: 978-0-6486816-6-3

Cover design by Robert New

Tale Publishing
Melbourne, Australia

Tale

A magical world helps stall the inevitable darkness.

Arcobar Yarns

No summer lasts forever. Yet from memory, my last summer at *Arcobar* was exactly that – it lingered and lingered until my time ran out, my working life truly over.

But let me not get ahead of myself...

For sure, you'd wish to know who's talking. Right then, here goes... It's Dervla, a name I suppose that's somewhat unfamiliar to your tongue. And before you confuse me with the other waitress, Marita, I'll spell out what I look like. Just a little on the short and stout side, I confess, with a pitted face that's put up with 50 years of wind, rain and scorching summers. Short-cropped silver hair. Sort of attractive *inside out*. And oh, there's my wind-chime earrings, of course, to go with my pale blue eyes. Spot them and you'd have spotted me – that's if you've ever detoured into the *Arcobar* for coffee, drinks or a super pizza. Or taken in a show like *Beatles Remembered.*

But for now ... I'm sitting cosy like in my kitchen before my faithful oil radiator (a Bunning's Hardware bargain) with a rug over my knees. Monday 10 am. Kettle on the boil. Tim Tams laid out. Keenly waiting. Waiting for Wendy, the nice lady volunteer. It'll be her first visit to get me started on my book – not her *reading* to me. No. But me telling *her* stories. Spinning yarns of heart, hope and humour. As for Wendy… she'll record me on her phone and later transcribe all my yarns into a pretty booklet. How exciting is that! Confess, I'm a little nervous. That's to be expected, I guess.

I've Irish blood you see, my family name's Kelly, going all the way back to *Ned Kelly*. No jokes, I'm historical. Ned's dad, the story goes, was shipped to Australia in 1840 just for helping himself to a couple of pork chops, as potatoes were becoming a scarcity. Reason why I can't resist hot chips.

There's Wendy now, bursting in like an early spring morning, excitement that fills the air, a spray of lavender deodorant. My nervousness goes out the window. Wendy quickly explains the technical process. 'I can manage that,' I say, relief lighting up my face.

After some chit chat over English breakfast tea and a nibble, we make ourselves comfortable, and I get started with my first story…

Soulful Eyes

There's this time... a late Sunday at *Arcobar* when we'd closed and had done with cleaning up. I carted the scullery bin to the skip around the back. Overcast, creepy with shadows shifting in a chilly breeze. Nervy night sounds. You know what I mean, right? Anyway, I tell myself, *c'mon gal do the bloody thing and get back in.*

Someone had left the skip partially opened, you see. Lucky for me, I think, as I lean in and tip the waste into the dark steel pit. I do it quickly, before the dunny-like stench knocks me off my feet.

Almighty shit! A violent shiver grips me. I drop the bin and scream. Brushing my hair furiously, I run back into the scullery almost knocking over Kung Foo. His real name's Foo but we prefer his nickname.

'What tha hell?' he says in a shrill voice. 'You see tha ghost or somthin?'

I'm still shaking, tongue-tied.

Kung Foo's the chef at *Arcobar* on two days when it's *walk-in-wok-time* — noodle and fried rice dishes, and such like. He's Chinese from Vietnam, a boat survivor. Wily old bugger, tall, lean and weathered with a wispy beard. Some say he's a spitting image of Ho Chi Minh, the Vietcong leader who spooked the cocksure Yankees. Foo isn't flattered.

I see Wendy glancing at her phone. A momentary frown, as if hinting I get on with the meat of my story, not piss around.

Kung Foo sits me on a stool, I continue, and gets me a glass of water. Then gently prompts me as he's taking off his dirty apron.

'Now what this big fright about, eh?'

Two other kitchen staff, changed and ready to set off, hesitate, curious to eavesdrop.

'A creepy-crawly something from the skip jumped me,' I say in a jittery voice, and demonstrate: 'Runs up my shoulder, back of my neck and onto my head. Gone in a flash. Something larger than a king roach.'

'What, what that you say?' Foo leans into my face with incredulous eyes.

'Much smaller than a possum,' I add, feeling the shivers again and goosebumps on my arm.

Wendy bursts out laughing like she guesses what's coming. 'What?' I say, feeling tickled myself.

'Should have warned you,' says Kung Foo his face wrinkling with amused sympathy.

'Eh?' I'm puzzled like he's playing a joke on me.

'It's the *Year of the Rat*, Dervla. You must know that. It's when rats and mice bring us great prosperity.'

'What prosperity?' Of course, I'm confused and stare at him. Then it hits me. A shit-scared mouse, that's all it was. A *frickin* little thing gave me such a monster fright.

I sit there feeling all stupid and foolish – and angry at the same time with bloody Foo.

'Hey, that's a real funny one, Dervla. Is that it then?' says Wendy all smiles, about to turn off the recording.

'No, no, the story's not done yet. In fact, it gets better, much better,' I laugh out loud, and a fit of coughing takes me, quite alarming Wendy.

'You right there?'

'All good,' I say not mentioning my painful mouth ulcers, side effect of treatment. I excuse myself and duck into the loo, then grab myself a cold glass of milk. Wendy turns on the recording as soon I'm seated again, blanket on knees.

Wendy's jacket lies crumpled beside her.

In a few days, I quite forget the episode and go about happily welcoming my regular customers who, thank God, are returning to *Arcobar* after Covid. Then one dinner time *shit hits the fan*. A seated male customer turns up at the counter after visiting the loo, looking not too pleased. Boris, serving drinks, looks up all friendly.

'A repeat, mate?'

'Who's in charge here?' scowls the man.

'Oh!' Boris hears alarm bell.

'Sorry but Monty's not in just now, mate. Can I help?'

'Listen here. Don't *mate* me,' hisses the customer, hostility in his eyes. 'How come a fuckin dirty mouse is hanging about the gents, eh? Scandalous! We're getting out right now, my wife and kids. And don't expect me to pay.'

'But...but...' Boris is totally flummoxed. 'You be mistaken, mate. No rodent pests here. We're a respectable joint.'

'Hey, don't mess with me,' he threatens leaning into the counter, giving Boris a puff of venom. 'I'll see you lose your licence.'

I'm standing, mouth open, just a table away with two plates of steak and chips.

Next thing, he strides out fuming, his wife and kids in tow, looking confused and distressed. We're left with half-eaten plates. Our regulars look up curiously: *What's up? What's with them, eh?*

When boss Monty returns from his weekend cross-country skiing, he summons us all to a full-blown interrogation session.

Jacob, the casual teenage kitchenhand, a South Sudanese migrant, lets the cat out of the bag. Yeah, he's seen Foo put out a plate of nibbles at the skip. Even admitting that *he* does it on days Foo's away – convinced he too will be rewarded big time by the *good luck rat God.*

'What, there's more of them vermin out there?' screams the boss, his face almost red as ketchup. 'Go and fetch bloody Foo right away,' Frightened, Jacob bolts on his giraffe-like legs. Fortunately, you see, the chef lives only a few streets away, above a shoe repair shop owned by his son.

'This is madness', Monty continues, pacing before us. Some of us try very hard to suppress a giggle.

'They'll shut us down, you know that. And we'll be out of a job.'

Foo turns up all apologetic, bowing as if he's praying to the god of compassion, which seems to incense Monty all the more. He instructs Foo to get a pest controller right away and sort out the pesty problem. Twenty-four hours is all the time he's given. 'And' he adds, 'you'll be digging into your pocket to sort out the mess.'

Foo looks conflicted and mortified. He pleads that the pest control people will only poison his poor mice. He can't allow that to happen – not in the *Year of the Rat*. Between tears he appeals to be given time to move them far away – safely. 'I pray good luck for you, boss Monty, and great prosperity for *Arcobar*.'

I feel sorry for Foo and, at risk to my own job, tell Monty that Foo has a point. Cruelty to harmless creatures will not do his soul any good. St Peter may not let him through the heavenly gates. A few staff, eyes down, nod hesitatingly. That seems to stun Monty. He clenches and releases his fist. After a long pause he decides.

'Okay, all of you who feel sorry for this bugger, help him dispose of the mice, rats or whatever. Dervla, for sticking out your neck, I put you in charge. Yours will be the first head to roll, in case…'

Jacob and I are the only ones to stick around. Others leave, either indifferent to Foo's plight or cynical about his *Year of the Rat* nonsense. Or they simply dread rodents.

By the time Foo returns with a wire cage from the Shanghai two-dollar shop, it's quite dark, overcast, and nippy.

Why such a large cage I ask. A grave stare is all I get. Foo's too preoccupied setting it up. Jacob and I stand close observing him kneeling near the skip and carefully preparing the trap, using bits of cheese and blobs of peanut butter.

'Eh, mice love peanut butter? News to me,' exclaims Wendy chuckling. *'So do I...'*

Foo, Jacob and I return to the kitchen and wait. But Foo's not up to small talk to pass the time. He lights up a couple of incense sticks and sticks them in a banana, then squats on a low stool rocking gently, muttering words in Chinese. It makes me uncomfortable. To give him some respectful space, I move away to get myself a mug of coffee. Jacob follows meekly.

Suddenly, Foo jumps up and rushes out, but returns in a minute shaking his head. False alarm. We sit some more. I'm yawning, my useless frustrated thoughts all over the place.

Jacob, squatting on the floor, back to the wall, is nodding off, head lolling on his chest.

Near 11 pm, Foo runs out for the fifth time, then calls out excitedly. We rush to him. He has the cage raised in his hand. 'See, see! My rat family all here. Take photo, take photo for boss, right.'

'What? Five at one go. That's incredible,' I say staring. The poor things cower, huddled in the partial light - three littlies and two decent sized mice. One fixes me with soulful, beady eyes. Shame, poor thing. Very likely the mummy, shit scared of what's to become of her babies. The woeful look quite unnerves me.

Foo just grins and grins, his eyes ablaze. '*Guin Yin* help me.' I learn much later that Guin Yin was the god of compassion.

We three drive to *Kamarooka Park* and let the mice loose. They virtually fly out of the cage, disappearing together into the thicket. My heart's pounding, my eyes welling. Jacob shakes his head knowingly. 'Ah, they're happy to be free – just like me.'

Foo keeps his job. The popularity of his dishes kept growing – so too the reputation of *Arcobar*. Monty increases the *wok menu days* to four.

In some secret way Foo makes sure no more mice are ever spotted – at least for the time he remains at *Arcobar*.

Then one evening in December, after we'd closed, Monty gathers us all together and serves us glasses of wine, hands us a Christmas bonus. A surprising announcement follows. An entrepreneur from Hong Kong has made an irresistible offer to buy the business - treble its market value. 'A bloody killing for the owners,' he says

Foo is away in Vietnam at the time paying homage to his deceased parents. Had he been here, I think he'd say knowingly: *That's a big happy thanks to you, boss Monty, from my rat family. See how Guin Yin, my god of mercy, makes miracles.*

'Hey, that's one super yarn,' says Wendy brightly as she drops her phone into her hessian bag. What should I call this story?'

'Mmm... perhaps Soulful Eyes. How's that?'

Yeah, sounds about right. I'm so keen to hear your next story though. Simply can't wait a whole fortnight.'

'Depends,' I say feeling very tentative. 'I have trouble remembering these days, can't get my

brain working.' Guess I'd have to improvise if the push comes to shove, I think, wing it like. I'd do almost anything to have Wendy keep coming. Living alone isn't much fun.

A Cat with Attitude

You know people had it bloody awful during the covid lockdown. Especially kids who vegetated at home shut off from school and their best friends. Rotten for me as well because Arcobar, too, was closed for months.

'Yeah, a bloody grim time,' agreed Wendy. 'But thank God, all things pass.'

'No, you're mistaken there,' I say, 'Covid is still snooping around, always in different disguises, or flitting about like invisible ghosts of bad guys evicted from hell.'

'That's a hilariously grotesque picture,' says Wendy with a chuckle.

Okay, but here's a story worth recording.

~

One weekday evening during a lull at *Arcobar*, Marita and I sneak out to the back for a smoke. We make ourselves comfy on a couple of old wooden crates. We natter about this and that. You know how it is, us women never run out of gossip and gripes.

The next thing Marita complains about her sleep problem, which has only worsened since Covid hit. She's about given up on the endless home remedies suggested by concerned friends and family. Her frequent nightmares are a *nightmare*!

'Yeah,' I say, tutting. 'That's not good.'

She tells me that one evening, she and her man were watching Channel Nine News when the Premier, Daniel Andrews, came on to talk about Covid. Looking grave and severe as if he were the principal of a high school about to tension ill-disciplined pupils, he laid it on the line

'I'm sorry, but because some thoughtless people ignored my stay safe message, all of you will now have to wear the additional pain of a stage 4 lockdown from midnight tonight.'

Marita says she felt incensed and shouted at the tv screen. 'Hey, you can't do that. Aren't we in Melbourne, supposedly *the most liveable city*?' Her husband's only reaction was 'Calm down, dear. The Premier's only doing his job.'

Marita adds that it was easy for her husband as he was a big fan of the Andrews guy. But she found politics a pain in the backside.

After that announcement she went to bed fearful and frustrated. Tossed and turned much of the night, dozing only fitfully, troubled by a recurring nightmare. Alien capsules from outer space floating down from the night sky landing across the landscape. Each resembled a bloated red coronavirus, complete with deadly spikes. Marita feared they'd split open and let-loose octopus-like creatures programmed to syphon the breath out of earthlings.

She tumbled out of bed the next morning, still drowsy and drained. While squatting in the loo, she continues, she tried to psyche herself: *Get real, Marita, or you'll go batty. Why let Covid rattle you!*

~

The next morning was shrouded in a gloomy wintry chill. Marita says she decided to venture out and take in some exercise. She didn't wish to go bonkers shut in all day. Fresh air would do her good. Why waste her exercise hour, the daily outdoor freebie bestowed upon every citizen by Mr Andrews, the benevolent dictator!

I stare at Marita sitting near me feeling a little amused at her earnestness. There wasn't time to light up another smoke.

Motivated, she says, she set a steady pace along Corona Street. A large ginger cat suddenly appeared on the footpath ahead and ambled towards her. Nothing unusual, she told herself, paying it little attention. In her experience, any sensible cat will likely veer off with the approach of a human. But not this one. No, this ginger feline thing didn't bugger off, but rather sauntered nonchalantly closer and closer towards her. Marita felt a little bewildered, irritated, and vaguely uneasy. She slowed her pace, pretending not to notice. The cat brushed past with total indifference, without giving an inch. *Can you believe that Dervla! A cat with attitude*! It stayed its course, flouting the social distancing rule. Marita says she adjusted her facemask and sneaked a glance behind her, hoping to see the cat disappear into someone's property. But no, it didn't. The bloody thing stalled, confronting her on the footpath, staring fixedly with inscrutable menace. Marita quickened her pace, then broke into a run, feeling a sudden urge to be safely home. Once through the gate, she yanked off her facemask, now panting with sudden exhaustion laced with panic.

'You okay, dear?' inquired her husband, frowning with concern as he watered a pot-plant on the veranda.

Marita says she felt confused and foolish, pretended she hadn't heard him, and simply collapsed onto a garden bench. She had to lean over for a minute or two to slow her thumping heart, to breathe easy again. 'Hey Dervla, you can't guess how bloody scary it was. There was this moment when I feared that my precious breath would take off for good.'

'Go on,' I say with vague unease. 'You exaggerate, right? After all, Marita, it was just a cat that spooked you.'

She glares at me. 'You know that wise bloke Shakespeare? Well, he believed that when ordinary birds and animals act in strange and unusual ways, it is a sign, a warning of something terrible to come – a *grave* event. It's like how they say: if you hear an owl hoot, someone close is likely to die.'

Wendy smiles all sceptical. 'Go on,' she says.

Do you know, Marita actually found herself uneasily glued to TV news that evening and scanned next morning's *Herald Sun* for reports of strange and inscrutable happenings, for further sightings of prowling ginger cats. What is more, just to clinch her story and win me over, she tells me that her Nanna from country Victoria phoned late the next day, very upset. A feral cat had invaded her chicken run in the dead of night, killed her prized Lamborghini rooster.

Wendy shakes her head. 'What a load of rubbish. Surely not in this day and age?

'That may be so,' I say, 'but here's the thing: according to Shakespeare, that guy of infinite wisdom, there are more things in heaven and earth than you and I can ever imagine.

Shadow Man

Now that I've already narrated a couple of stories to Wendy, I readily slide into a kind of routine. So, once she's settled and has her recorder turned on, I start my next yarn.

One afternoon, as I half-doze before my radiator, the image of a man takes form in my mind, a mug-face in a dish of murky water. Quite weird, actually. It startles me because I remember him as a regular customer from my stint at *Arcobar*. A dark scruffy-faced guy in his forties, always in orange tradies safety vest and knocked-about worker's boots. Could be Fijian, could be an Islander. But then I'm no authority on dark-skinned people. But wait…, is there a touch of an *outback* drawl as he checks the menu and orders – a voice not unlike that of the detective in the tv series *Mystery Road*?

In any case, this guy keeps turning up for beer and a burger. An *Arcobar* special deal with dill pickle. Around 9 pm mostly, just when I'm killing yawns, done on my feet and ready to call it a day. But still, there he is…

He prefers a table overlooking a vacant lot which runs along the length of our veranda with open-air seating. This block of land is, at least to me, an eye-score, an expansive ditch covered in wild grass and a isolated bush or two. Strewn with boulders, suspect they from elsewhere. And ankle-deep in water most times when it rains. Superstitious Marita, however, cautions me. 'Hey, don't say *eye-sore* out loud. Maybe a reason why it's left like it is.'

'Like what?' I ask, certain she's pulling my leg, you know. But then the look on her face tells me she really means it. 'Maybe it's a *sacred site* or something – with even a curse on it.'

Whatever, I think, laughing it off. The customers' kids seem not to notice, though. They turn it into a *fun park*, have a rollicking time running up and down the grassy slopes, screaming and mucking about.

For some odd reason, the tradie always adjusts his chair to face this vacant patch. Puzzles me no end. He nods when I come to take his order and nods when leaving. Nibbles and sips with a morose faraway look. Never so much as a word –

except once he gives me this cryptic half smile when he orders. One time I offer him my name and comment on the shitty weather.

'Called Archie by me mates,' he returns in a voice gone husky with excess of beer and smokes. 'Like Uncle Archie Roach,' he adds after a pause, like he's giving me a hint of something. Oh, and another thing: I never see him pull out a phone. Never ever.

Archie keeps coming the whole of that year. Then stops. Abruptly. No mystery in that I tell myself. Guess he may have worked on a nearby building site, a short-term roads project or some such job. When done, he's just moved on. Happens all the time – even here mostly with the casuals.

'Mmm,' say Wendy 'a guy with intrigue, like that strong silent bloke Shane. Remember the movie by the same name? You've seen it, right?

'Yeah,' I say. Not letting on I never go to movies. Never did. I do wonder, though, how people seem to appear and disappear in my life, even a few regulars at Arcobar. Somewhat sad really, you know. But to continue…

Archie becomes one of my more interesting customers. So, it's understandable why I couldn't stop myself from speculating about his life, his family connections and what kept him going. But he's disappeared now, and that's that.

With the busy goings on at *Arcobar*, Archie soon evaporated from my mind like he never existed. A case of *out of sight, out of mind*. Exactly why I'm floored when the bugger drifts in again one chilly wet evening. Almost a year on, most unexpected, mind you. The kitchen's about to close. I'm irritated that he comes this late expecting to be served

Yes, you guessed right. Archie walks straight to his favourite table overlooking the vacant lot, now bathed eerily in moonlight. He stands and stares out. 'Same again Archie?' I ask coming up close behind him. Isn't in his usual tradie's vest this time and gives off a peculiar smell like accumulated rat shit.

He turns and looks at me as if uncertain of my question, his eyes strangely dull. Maybe high on drugs, I think, which I detest like hell. I take off to fetch his usual - an *Arcobar* burger and a glass of chilled Victoria bitters.

'Didn't you ask him about his time away?' says Wendy.

'No, how could I? That's like being personal.

In any case, with that Northern Territory drawl, you see, he may even have gone on a walkabout.

I return with his meal in fifteen minutes only to find him still glued to the window. Now I'm becoming more than a little annoyed. I'm held up from all that scullery mess needing attention. So, I step up and say with firm politeness that we are closing in five minutes. No response. I'm about to tap him on the shoulder and say *hey!* when I feel a needle-prick pain on my arm. *Ouch!* I fall back thinking it's a cramp. In that moment, Archie turns, his eyes meeting mine, a fleeting cryptic smile.? I'm left bewildered and unsettled as he glides out without a word, his meal untouched and unpaid for.

I dump the uneaten order in the scullery. The casual hand wonders aloud why I look a little pale and shaken. I say nothing.

'Now, Wendy, you not gonna believe the sequel. Yes, there's certainly one ...'

'Go on, go on...I'm all ears.'

Well, on Friday of that week, an hour before opening for lunch, who should call on us unannounced, but two cops, fresh-faced in their police-issue blue uniform and distinct cap. Raised eyebrows all around, they did. They chatted with

Monty out of earshot. Next thing the boss calls out.

'Hey there, just a moment,' he says to us laying out the tables. 'Marita, Dervla call the others from the kitchen.' This ought to be interesting, I think. The others exchange *what's-up* glances.

Monty clears his throat. 'Listen folks, these good officers need our assistance. Let's hear them out.'

Then the lady officer speaks up in a matter-of-fact fashion. She tells us that a male in his forties from Alice Springs, on temporary work here, was reported missing about twelve months ago. No leads until now. His battered blue Lancer sedan was located stripped and dumped in dense wetland near Nar Nar Goon. A blood-stained safety vest together with company ID pass in the hip pocket - and an *Arcobar* meal receipt.

The officer urges us to study the receipt to see if it rings a bell. She gives it to the boss. Sceptical murmurings. Receipt a year old! *Give us a break.* A fat chance of anyone recalling anything.

'Yeah, yeah, a long shot, I know,' cuts in Monty. 'But give it a go,' he encourages.

I feel oddly hesitant.

The receipt is passed from hand to hand. It's glanced at cursorily and passed on with a *nah*. Then it's my turn. One look and I feel suddenly woozy as if caught in a washing machine in a spin cycle. Monty grabs me as I knock into a chair. Great consternation. Staff crowd me, alarmed. Curious and concerned.

The lady officer sticks her eager face into mine. 'You recognise it?'

I nod feebly.

'Yeah?'

'Always had the same,' I whisper, '*Arcobar* burger and Victoria bitters.'

'So, you the one served him, right? The last time was on the day this receipt is dated.'

'No ma'am,' I whisper hardly able to get my voice out. 'He's come two days ago, the Wednesday past.' I break into a spasm, my hands in a cold sweat.

'Marita, get her some water,' calls out Monty with an incredulous look. 'You mean, two days ago, Dervla? You sure?

I stare at him. The terror in my eyes all too obvious. A scary feeling spreads like toxic fumes promptly unsettling the entire staff.

'Phew!' sighs Wendy. 'I can certainly do with

a cuppa.'

The break does me good. Being a little on the superstitious side myself, retelling the story meant like reliving a real nasty dream. Wendy's home baked scones are a welcome diversion. But still, having started the story, to escape finishing it, is no option. Wendy turns on the recording...

The boss is kind enough to give me two weeks break on full pay. Even so, I'm not overly excited waitressing there anymore. I have this fear that Archie might turn up again at a whim. Can't trust the dead, you know.

'Gee, that's really spooky. So, he was definitely murdered, right?'

'Well, I had to provide a full written statement about his last visit. The cops must have thought me nutty. But I'm told, they, nevertheless, spent days digging up the vacant lot. That's once it dried up and no longer marshy. Just in case... Do you know the cops actually found a few body parts. DNA confirmed it was Archie's. The remains, I'm told, were sent to his family for a traditional burial. What's more, the cops even unearthed clues at the site, which led them to the killer. Poor bugger, I hope that's given Archie and his family closure.

I now think he may have come to *Arcobar* for a purpose. Not sure what exactly. Maybe that strange departing smile of his conveyed a message. *Hey, Dervla, I've done my job, now you do yours.* I was too dumb then and too eager to clean up and get home. I feel rotten thinking about it.

Anyway, I quit *Acorbar* not long after. Was about to start a job in aged care. That's when I was diagnosed with this shit of an illness.

A fit of coughing comes over me. Wendy takes this as a sign she's perhaps overstayed.

'Can I help prepare your lunch before leaving?' she says with helpful concern.

'No, no need. Thanks, but I'm okay. Really.'

'Last thing then. What will we call this yarn? Stranger Danger or Shadow Man?'

'Shadow Man, Wendy. Let's hold onto that unless I come up with a better one.

Claddagh Love

I'm staring at the street through the netted curtains. Ah, there she comes. Twenty minutes late. Wendy steps out from her green Toyota, lifts her Woollies bag from the back seat, pats the front of her slightly crumpled dress. I smile. When we're finally seated, I couldn't resist saying'

'Why Wendy, you're looking great, your nails simply gorgeous.'

'You like it? Thanks, spring always brings out a fresh feeling in me. Peach blossom pink. Guess I shouldn't indulge myself like this at my age.'

I glance at my calloused hands and change the subject.

'Come let's get us a cuppa.'

'Okay,' says Wendy happily, 'but sorry I was held up at the nail salon. Seems you're anxious to get started.'

Gosh, how easily my face gives me away. 'Yeah, been up early, worrying and waiting.' I say apologetically, resting my mug. 'Worry about this encroaching fog stealing more and more of my thoughts, my memories. But still…'

The other night I'm tossing and turning, feeling like dog shit, sleeping in bits and starts. I think I hear the blinds rattle as if I'd not quite shut the bedroom window. Can't be. I sit up. Only the sounds of stillness. The sickly pale streetlight steals in through chinks in the blinds. I try sleeping again, turning to rest my head the other way, my gliding eyes taking in the chair in the far corner.

Stomach lurches, leaping into my mouth. There's this old woman come uninvited, sitting in the shadows, a flicker of light picking up half her face, turning her eyes into distant stars. My tongue's frozen stiff. I can't look away. Definitely Maeve I tell myself, another of my one-time *Arcobar* patrons. Why doesn't she speak, say something? My eyes adjust, and I can tell she's in a drab floral nightgown, face as sullen as when I served her Irish stew on her special birthday. Hell, I pray she'd bugger off and leave me to catch some sleep.

It's such a relief when I awake later with sunlight dazzling my face. The chair in the corner vacant as always.

Wendy chortles and gives me a quizzical smile.

'You making this up, right? And that old woman's name is really Maeve? Not your late grandmother by any chance?'

I keep a straight face and shake my head emphatically. 'But do allow me to proceed.'

The first I lay eyes on Maeve is when her daughter arranges a birthday for her at *Arcobar*. It's her 70th, I'm told, although the woman, tall, stooped and frail, looks every bit near ninety. Reminds me of a cast-off piece of heritage furniture. A patterned blue scarf covers her head, tied under the chin. The name being Irish, Maeve gets my full sympathy. Poor woman, I think, remembering my nanna weighed down by a lifetime of grief during *The Troubles* – the bloody conflict when Catholics and Protestants were at each other's throats.

The daughter, her husband, their two children come to celebrate Maeve's milestone. They're joined by an Indian couple in flashy clothes – neighbours.

But here's the thing… Maeve, a fussy eater, had apparently insisted that she'd only attend her birthday if the menu includes traditional Irish stew. The others aren't that fussed. And that's exactly what the chef prepares – using a recipe texted us in advance by daughter, Karen. Of course, the birthday girl isn't to know. After all, it's a once-in-a-life time affair.

When they come, we're ready with a table laid out all colourful with flowers, tinsel and balloons tied to the chairs. Karen winks at me as I place before her mother a large bowl of chunky Irish stew - steaming hot. I hope no other patron, tantalised by the aroma, would say *I'll have what's she having*.

'Enjoy Maeve,' I say gifting her a broad smile. 'And a very special birthday wishes from me, Dervla, your Irish sister.' That gets her attention. She raises her wintery eyes with interest. A faint smile flickers and is quickly lost on an age-weathered face. She asks me where my family's from and when I'd come here. My, my, I think, now here's a real genuine *Irish brogue* my ears rarely encounter. I feel suddenly so ashamed of my Aussie twang.

I brag of my *Ned Kelly* lineage. But Maeve switches off as soon as she hears I'm Australian born. I leave her dipping into her soup. Karen mouths *thanks*. I guess it's the first time in a while her mum has smiled and shown interest in someone.

I turn and catch Monty's *c'mon get-a-move* stare. In the few minutes I'm with Maeve, many more patrons have been shown to tables. Pretty soon I'm running to and fro like a headless chook. But still, I keep a watchful eye on Maeve's table. I spot the old lady being helped to the *ladies*.

Just as three staff walk in from the kitchen with a candle-lit cake, singing happy birthday, consternation hits the table. Maeve's up on her feet wailing, wringing her hands in frantic distress, Karen's not able to console her. People seated nearby are distracted from their meals.

I'm standing open mouthed, vaguely hear Monty's voice reminding me: *You have other patrons to serve, Dervla. Leave the old lady to me*. Nothing about why the poor woman's upset. No...My boss can be a callous arsehole.

'Yeah, yeah, but tell me', says Wendy, 'I'm dying to hear the reason.'

I laugh at her childlike impatience. 'Hang on,' I say feeling a shiver. I tug at the blanket over my knees. 'Give my story a chance to get there, right.'

'Sorry.' She gives me an apologetic grin, removes her jacket and settles back in her chair.

I turn down the radiator - just a little.

Monty encourages Karen to leave since her frail mother seems far too unsettled to be pacified. As I pack the uncut birthday cake back into its box, the daughter explains that Maeve had got into a fit when she didn't see her wedding ring on her finger. Karen thinks it may be at home. Misplaced. She confides that it isn't the first time the heirloom ring had slipped off.

Will she take home the barely touched stew as well? 'Don't worry', she says. Her mum enjoyed the little she'd sampled. Asks that the chef be thanked for taking the trouble.

I hug Maeve, her face wet and woeful, and return to my other customers. But before then, I clean and re-set Maeve's table, leaving the bowl of chunky stew and other scraps in the scullery to chuck out later.

Wendy interrupts to say that many long-married older women tend to be passionately attached to their wedding rings – unlike the younger set who may marry many times over. I couldn't agree more.

It's a welcome surprise to see Maeve's daughter a few weeks later on a balmy Saturday afternoon. As I come out with a meal order in each hand, I catch her at the counter ordering drinks.

'Hey hello, you Karen, Maeve's daughter, right?'

She has brought her mother for tea and scones and, of course, to listen to the host band perform songs of the popular Irish band *Corr*.

'We're outside near where the band's playing. Come say hi to her.'

'Will do. I bring out the tray. And what about a teeny-weeny drop of Guinness to warm mum's cockles?'

'That's an idea,' she says, adding that Maeve remains down in the dumps, more so now that her wedding ring hadn't turned up at home, although they'd searched high and low. They now suspect it had fallen out at *Arcobar* – maybe even into the toilet bowl.

She urges me to tell workers to keep an eye out. A reward of $100 to anyone who finds it. I humour her for believing in miracles.

After the show, the daughter seats Maeve in the car and hastens over to find me. She sticks a picture of the precious ring into my hand. A *Claddagh*. 'I shouldn't be telling you this,' she whispers earnestly into my ear above the din. 'My dad was blown up in Derry during *The Troubles*. I never knew him. My mum in her late twenties then, heavily pregnant with me.'

'Holy Mary,' I gasp as she disappears out the door. Poor Maeve. How bloody awful. No wonder her nerves' all shot.

Being of Irish stock myself, I know a little about the *Claddagh*, a ring shrouded in centuries of Celtic myths and superstition. But in Maeve's case, the ring is painfully personal as well. And her losing it is catastrophic, a betrayal of her vow of eternal love for her beloved who was lost too soon, killed tragically.

I show Wendy a picture of the ring, a copy of the one Karen handed me at Acorbar for staff to see. Her eyes light up intrigued by the iconic design of two hands clasping a heart with a crown on top. With my hands I give you my heart crowned with love. Even now my chest goes tight when I think of Maeve, her unending pain.

'*You know, Dervla, if I were Karen, seeing how her mother suffers, I'd quietly replace the ring with a new one.*'

Maeve knew *her* ring as no other. Why? Because of a distinct hairline fracture at the rim, happened when she fell off her husband's bike riding pillion. Newly married, they were returning from church.

I'm beginning to tire. Stop flogging the story, I tell myself. Have done with it. I also sense Wendy's eager to know the ending.

Well, the $100 reward really gets *Acorbar* staff pumped up. A challenge like who would hit the jackpot. Marita, however, isn't that sure. 'Some things lost are never *meant* to be found', she says, like she's a *know-all*. 'Definitely not a ring smeared with medieval mumbo-jumbo stuff.' Her doubt is infectious. Soon the enthusiasm among workers falters and ebbs.

But then one Saturday evening late, as we're about finished with the cleaning and setting up for the next day, young Rubio, a Tafe student and casual cleaner, comes bursting in speechless, his eyes on fire, his hand in the air holding something between thumb and finger. I scream: 'Jesus, it's the ring, the ring.'

We rush him shocked and disbelieving. I grab the ring and examine it closely for the fracture. It's certainly it. But where outside *Arcobar* could he have found it? Others take turns in examining the incredible find. So, this is a *Claddagh*, right? Well, I never…

I shove Rubio into a chair and demand an explanation, convinced he'd picked up the ring on the night Maeve dropped it in *Arcobar*, returning it now only to claim the reward.

'No, no it's not true,' he pleads. I demand he explains himself, exactly how he come by the ring. Here's his response – a miracle if ever there is one to outdo all others. 'The vet found it in the stomach of my black Labrador,' he says.

'Hey Rubio, don't bullshit us,' people shout almost in unison. But he looks up with appealing eyes, adamant. Sticks like glue to his *believe-it-or not* story.

Yeah, I recall, I've seen his Labrador, Guzzle, come a few times with Rubio. Spotted him snoozing at the back door near the skip. Not my favourite breed. Forever faking hunger, bolting down almost anything their eyes or noses pick up.

Well, when Rubio spotted an almost full bowl of Irish stew in the scullery going to waste, he naturally saved it and took it home for Guzzle, who licked it clean. And wanted more! The rest is history.

'C'mon, Dervla don't short-change me. The details please - no matter how absurd it may sound. I indulge Wendy – reluctantly.

Rubio tells us that in the fortnight following that sumptuous feed, the dog became ever more listless. His mum began to worry when Guzzle gave up on food. Initially, the vet treated him with doggie *pep-me-up* pills. But then an x-ray showed a small blockage in the stomach. Surgery followed. The vet was certain that what he'd removed was no more than a tightly matted ball of hair and fine carpet fibres. But failing to slice it open, he set about pulling the lump apart with his hands and uncovered a metal object. He almost fell off his high stool to discover it was really a rather strange-looking ring.

Wendy laughs raucously, almost to the point of tears. She shuts off the recording, gives me a quick hug before picking up her bag. I grimace as I close the door, swallow two Panadol and steal into the bedroom for a lie down.

Made in Heaven

I'm ready for Wendy when she returns a fortnight later. Even managed to bake a few Anzac bikkies to impress.

I've always been fortunate in having warm and friendly neighbours. That's until a year ago.

There's this house opposite... two spinster sisters in their late forties lived there. House sold now, being pulled apart for a radical facelift. I hope for a family with little kids to move in. Infuse new life to the street.

Cathy and Sue were real characters. I really miss them - especially now that I'm virtually housebound. I picture them romping in and out most days to check on me, bringing along baked goodies and female gossip. Sue now lives in Mornington close to her brother, while Cathy, by a strange quirk of fate, became a *born-again woman* – her words not mine. It's a story worth telling.

Cathy is the flamboyant one with tinted hair and colourful new-age clothes. Happened after a trip to Nimbin. You know that outlandish hippie town in NSW, once a tourist mecca. Sue, for her part, is too caught up with her cycling buddies and fretting over various aches and pains. Cathy is lonely and says she mostly talks to the walls.

They both enjoy coming to shows at *Arcobar*. Drink a lot and generally get themselves into a serious jolly mood – too raucous and silly for some customers. Uber is a godsend for them – and a relief for me as one who worries over their safety. Monty knows exactly when to approach their table, sweet-talk them on their way.

The problem is they seem to get on each other's nerves, especially after several glasses of Chardonnay. Then it becomes time to air dirty linen in public. Quite embarrassing really. At times I interrupt my work to walk one of them to the *ladies* and back, to cool things before a wine glass gets flung.

There was this one time when a group called *Scatterings,* two guys and a girl, came to perform songs of Dolly Parton and Kenny Rodgers. Sue and Cathy claimed the table nearest the band stand.

The girls, saturated with Chardonnay, began playing up in their own fashion, competing with the singers. Their high pitched and off-key voices irritate customers no end. I was about to step in and *shush* them when one of the guys in the band, the lanky hairy-faced one, rested his guitar and stepped down to Cathy. His mates continued performing. I feared he was about to slap her for being wilfully disruptive. But you know what?

'Yeah, what? I'm all ears.' Wendy's eyes shine with amused curiosity.

'He bowed like a perfect gentleman and stretched out a chivalrous hand. Cathy took the cue, all giggles. They waltzed to *Islands in the Stream* in slow uncertain motion in the tight space between the tables and the bandstand. A few more people stood up behind their chairs and swayed to the music. Some patrons cheered and clapped. Waitering staff stopped a moment to watch. Even now I feel the passing joy I felt then.

It didn't surprise me a bit when Marty and Cathy hit it off and began dating. But I was floored when Cathy came screaming to my place one morning two months later to announce that Marty had proposed. That's bloody sudden I told myself. Bloody remarkable. I cautioned Cathy to allow the relationship to mature a little, not to rush into marrying.

'No, no you don't understand, Dervla,' she said. 'It's his wife that's made it happen.'

'C'mon,' I said incredulous like. 'What you mean? You pulling my leg, right? Marty's wife's *kaput*, not exactly around to arrange a substitute girl for her hubby.'

'No, not joking Dervla. Never been more serious.'

'Okay, convince me then. This I'd like to hear.' We sat in the kitchen. I helped myself a tot of brandy, neat. I waited. Cathy was sweating. Don't ask me why. Maybe she was still recovering from the shock of being asked, her rare good fortune.

Well, the story goes that Marty told Cathy that it was no accident they met when they did. He believed it was providence, fate, destiny… whatever.

'You see, my dear wife died in an accident years ago, and I've been desperately lonely since. Makes my late wife very sad, you see. So, she hunts around and finds you. Now she's very happy. Exceedingly so.'

Cathy said she continued staring at Marty open mouthed, not quite getting it, her head in a tizz.

'My Clint Eastwood look-alike, takes me by

the hand saying, *See, love, me late wife's name was Katie, celebrated her birthday on 15 November.*'

'Bugger me,' I blurted out, 'This is unreal. And you're *Cathy* born on *15 November!*' I really don't know what to make of it. Don't exactly believe in miracles. A weird coincidence more likely. Whatever. But no doubting, it was truly *a match made in heaven*.

I enjoy Wendy's visits as much as she seems to enjoy my yarns. Secretly though, I must admit it's becoming an effort for me to keep going. It's terribly exhausting. Of course, I know deep down that the fun we're having will not last much longer...

Lord of Dance

The view from my bedroom is simply gorgeous. What a joy. A compact garden of lavender and jasmine, with a camelia bush as backdrop. I hesitate to say that the display's enough *to take my breath away* just in case *Mr Grim Reaper,* misunderstands and turns up sooner than expected.

I've moved home. So here I am propped up in bed at the Nellie Melba Hospice in Frankston. I've handed over my future to a caring palliative team, passing my days and nights mostly dozing. No complaints.

Expecting Wendy soon. This visit will likely be her last, a curtain drawn on our project – my stories of heart, hope and humour recorded for posterity. Yeah, sounds just too good. To hold a book spruiking my name, a product of illustrious *Office Works*. How good is that! Hey, I'll call myself a *writer* then.

Wendy bursts in with a bright smile. She takes in the airy room and the sunlit view framed by the window, throws her scarf briskly over the back of the chair and rests her basket close at hand.

'Let's see if this works.' She places her phone on my lap and turns on the recorder. So, what will you be yarning about today?'

Well... I was thinking about when the men's toilet at Arcobar flooded on Christmas Eve and Monty fell and messed his fancy Christmas outfit.

'Yeah, that would be quite hilarious. But...' She eyes me closely. I couldn't quite conceal how sick I feel behind my mock cheerfulness.

'Wouldn't you rather tell the story of how you persuaded Arcobar to celebrate your wake? Now, that was not just hilarious but damn hysterical. I for one hadn't heard of such a preposterous leg-pulling event before.

Yeah, why hadn't I thought of that. That would strike exactly the high note on which I could wrap up my precious sessions with Wendy. The icing on the cake. So I get started, telling as much as I recall.

I'm not sure how the idea first entered my mind. Just that in recent months I'd begun to wonder more and more what people I've known or been close to would say of me when I'm gone. Mostly good things, I hoped. The thought kept whirling in my head. Then I land here at Nellie

Melba.

In any case, one day three workers from *Arcobar* visited me bearing gifts, a get-well card, a bunch of daffodils and an envelope with cash - three hundred and fifty dollars. I felt taken aback by this unexpected gesture. Made me all emotional and teary. To think they'd spontaneously decided on a collection for me. For me! Even recent staff who'd not known me, chipping in. And Monty, would you believe it, doubled the taking. How could I ever thank them enough? Gave me a sleepless night or two. That's what sowed the idea of celebrating my life with people who truly mattered.

You know, I didn't really have need for the money. Not like I could take it with me - the way ancient Egyptians believed.

What if I reinvested the $350 in *Arcobar*? A big bash was just the thing. A kind of mock wake. The more I entertained the idea, the more excited I got. Yeah, close the joint for an evening. Get Monty to *shut shop* so every worker could come and let their hair down.

I confided in Cathy about my hidden motive. Both of you were highly sceptical. Remember? But thankfully, you humoured me. Cathy thought it a bizarre idea, but something already dreamt of by others - and successfully executed. That certainly spurred me on.

I phoned Monty to thank him for the thoughtful generosity of *Arcobar*. And thanked him, too, for the wonderful time I had working under him. Then, in the same breath, I asked if he would consider allowing me to celebrate my time there. But careful not to dump too many details of my plan on him at once. My wish, I explained, was that a few former staff may be invited - like chef Kung Foo. I assured him that I'd pay for everything. Monty went quiet for a moment. 'I'll let you know, okay. Meantime take care, Dervla.' He seemed vaguely hesitant as if I'd put him on the spot. My excitement dropped a notch.

Wendy yawns, her eyes glancing at the open door. I apologise for being long-winded No worries, she says, urging me to keep going for a little longer. She worries that the nursing staff may step in soon and send her packing, before totally exhausting me.

Two workers from *Arcobar* turn up unexpectedly a few days later - Sasha and Brett. Monty sends them to negotiate with me, giving them some leeway. It's funny, but these two were strangers to me, and almost half my age.

Jeez, but they were enthusiastic, keen as mustard to please me. Personally, I thought the young ones were quite overawed stepping into a hospice and then sitting close to someone soon to join the *dear departed* club. 'Yeah, yeah,' they chimed, 'we're game for anything. You just name it.'

But then things got a little out of hand, one outlandish idea triggering another. They were in stitches. I joined in till my chest hurt. We agreed a *mock wake* would be the ultimate thing, a memorable event long remembered. But they worried that the idea may spook some staff. No, not if we kept the details under wrap. We strategized ways to ensure secrecy. Call it a party of surprises. Staff only need to know there's to be a celebration of my enjoyable years at *Arcobar*. A thank you bash.

Exhaustion surges over me like a sudden tsunami, knocking me back onto my pillow, frightening the shit out of Wendy. Her phone slips off me.

'Hey Dervla, you okay?' Her panicked voice rings vaguely in my ear. 'Hang on, I'll go get the

nurse.'

'No wait,' I whisper, *'Sorry, but I'm still here. It's the morphine that's draining. Give me five minutes.'*

The juicy bits of the mock celebration were clearly the highlights. Sadly, my recollection seemed to be faltering, the details fading fast, shadows creeping over.

Hey, pep up, I tell myself, *all's not lost. We'll get done with this story yet.*

I open my eyes to catch Wendy leaning over me, her face in a frown, perhaps checking my breathing.

'Whew, what a relief. But you better rest now and we'll finish recording the story the next time.'

'Okay by me. And what if I just stick to a few memorable moments that are still vivid in my mind, ones that tickle your fancy? How's that sound, Wendy?'

'Well... Maybe it's the only option we have. Yeah, let's do it. And thanks for not quitting on our project just yet.'

'You mean me dying before it's done and dusted, packaged and all, right?'

An apologetic smile passes over Wendy's face.

~

The next time she comes, Wendy finds me propped up and overly eager and waiting. The nurse looks grave as she hands me the morning's medication. 'You're too hyped up, dearie. Got to take it easy or you'll get yourself into strife.' I smile weakly assuring her she needn't worry.

I have selected a few party photos on my phone from a heap sent me by staff. Wendy is pleased and amused by them. 'Great. That's a start. Let's see how we go.'

'But you'll help me along and fill in whenever I'm uncertain, right?' I hold the Samsung in an unsteady hand leaning a little towards Wendy. Wendy places her phone on my lap, turns on the recording, and rests her one hand on it to ensure it doesn't slide away.

Here's the first photo. It's Kung Foo walking in from the kitchen with two serving bowls full of crisp dim sims and spring rolls. The sight of his mischievous grin is simply heart-warming. Really lifts my spirit. Doubted he'd be there. Someone clearly went the extra mile to locate him. He'd left even before I did, moving to the other side of town, bloody long way away from *Arcobar*. Foo's wearing an oriental tunic in the photo and has on one of those ridiculous chef's white hat, tall as a chimney pot.

Photo two is seriously funny – a shocker for some of the staff. You see these two workers on the side? It's Marita and Robin, wide-eyed and hands on mouth. They seem to be aghast. It's one taken by you, Wendy.

'Yeah, remember I drove you to the function and wheeled you in. No one anticipated to see you arrive this way, a bald head and a blanket covering your knees. Takes them a little while to get over the shock.'

Now the third photo: people in tongue-tied silence. Look at their faces. Me in the limelight announcing I'd come to deliver the eulogy for Dervla. I'd pulled out an imitation copper chalice from under the blanket on my knees, and you placed it on the table next to me. *All of Dervla's in there* I say aloud. I tap it. The vessel emits a bell-like sound that spreads like a wave across the room. The penny drops almost immediately. A flood of whispering and nervous giggles - and Monty's chuckle at the back that happily breaks the tension. A ripple of amused laughter, everyone relaxes.

I tell a few light-hearted stories of my memorable years at *Arcobar*. The one about Kung

Foo and his family of *good luck* mice had them hysterical. You see here in this photo, the red-haired woman standing slightly behind me? That's Cathy, once my neighbour and a regular at the restaurant at the time. She's the one who shacked up with a bloke in a band that performed at *Arcobar*. Well, Cathy steps up to thank me after I'd spoken. Yeah, I recall her words of praise: *Here's a woman with hell of a courage who dared to come to her own wake and deliver the eulogy.* People cheer and applaud. Foo bangs furiously on a small wok.

Whilst they are still roused and responsive, Sasha and Brett take over. The next three photos show them in action. In this one Sasha's enticing the staff to participate in a balloon activity while Brett is passing around a plastic takeaway container with balloons. See the clutch of eager hands. They're unaware then what's to follow. This next photo shows people with puffed cheeks and bulging eyes straining to blow their balloons to almost bursting point. Once done, they're instructed to twist the neck of the balloon and hold it firmly to prevent air escaping.

Now comes the trick. Patient Sasha is delighted when it's her turn again. 'Hold up your balloons in your left hand everybody, and let's see how well you've done. Wow! That's great. Now grab a toothpick from Brett with your other hand,' continues Sasha cheerfully. Chortles mixed with nervous giggles erupt. 'No, no, you don't prick your balloon, not just yet. But listen carefully to what Brett has to say.'

Brett jumps onto a stool. 'This is Dervla's wake. But she's chosen to celebrate her wake with all of us. It's her gift in return for what's *Acorbar's* given her. Dervla says *dying* is the name of this game – a certainty for all of us. No exceptions.' He pauses and looks at their puzzled faces, some anxious. 'Here's the thing. Dervla believes that none of us has control over how we go in the end. But this doesn't mean we can't *wish how we would like to leave this life:* spectacularly like a big cosmic bang or fizzle out in fear like a damp firecracker.'

Deathly silence. It's as if my blanket's suddenly come down over the heads of everyone in the room. 'Okay, wakey wakey.' Sasha rouses them. 'Now's the time for each of you to wish your very personal wish. To either *prick* your balloon or allow the air to *seep out slowly*. Go for it.'

Lots of ear-splitting popping amidst laughter and screams. A few balloons *swish* into the air.

A truly tear-welling moment for me. So uplifting!

'So *spiritual*,' says Wendy with a glint in her eyes.

I'm grateful that many captured the moment on their phones. Examining the photos sent, I'm struck by all the faces of daring and relief. It seems people got a real emotional buzz from this activity. I hope many will savour the memory of their experience. But then *forgetfulness* is the name of the rival game that rules our lives. Memory is such a fickle thing.

'Yeah,' adds Wendy, 'I recall how people came alive hugging and cheering. As for me, I really worried then, Dervla, the wheelchair would topple, and you'd be crushed by all the fierce embraces.'

We laugh in unison, recalling the absurdity of the situation. Yeah, I think, it was such fun. But now… A long silence intrudes. I shift, feeling a slight hip-strain from sitting propped up in one position. Wendy promptly rearranges the pillows.

Okay, here's my last selection of photos. Wendy leans over and looks at them. They're of

Marty and his band in dynamic poses rendering a lively number called, *Lord of the Dance*, a favourite of mine. The version by the *Dubliners* and Jim McCann is most catchy and captivating. I'd chosen it in the hope the celebrations would end on a high note. Closure on a jolly mood. I'm so pleased my hope was largely fulfilled.

Wendy says she recalls her blood flowing, her body moving. Intoxicating is her choice description. I never would have guessed that the Dubliners would get people into such a frenzy of passionate dancing - tossing arms, kicking legs and giddy whirling as if possessed. Even now I have this vision of a Celtic ritual at Stonehenge, a ritual perhaps to drive away the angel of death. Wow!

But when chairs begin toppling, I recall a look of alarm on Monty's face. 'Hey, watch it, he shouted over the din. 'Enough, that's quite enough for tonight. Pack it up

.'

I still hear the Dubliners, their refrain echoing in my mind, stoking hope in a grieving heart.

Dance, then, wherever you may be
I am the lord of the dance said he

And I lead you all wherever you may be
And I lead you all in the dance said he.

Gift to Last

This is Wendy here…

Dervla's book will not be properly done, I think, if I don't now step in to ensure the kind of closure it deserves. So, here's the bit about my dear friend's final moments.

I visited the hospice with an edited and formatted first draft of the stories, a bound *Office Works* copy. Despite her failing vision and depleted energy, Dervla clutched it to her chest, sniffed and felt it, opened the book, raised it close to her eyes. Her face lit up. She drew me close thanking me with a hug.

It's just then that Kung Foo turned up. What a lovely surprise. Dervla kept repeating his name as she clasped his hand. They laughed together.

'I come with luck for you,' he said cryptically. 'My granddaughter's pet come with me.' He reached into his inside jacket pocket and gently pulled out something. He smiled as he placed it on Dervla's chest.

I gasped.

Dervla felt it and squealed with delight, immediately recognising it. 'Wendy, see a friendly mouse,' she whispered, letting it crawl over her. The pet moved cautiously up towards Dervla's face. Stopped and sniffed the air, its pink nostrils in a quiver, then moved a little more. Dervla giggled and giggled as the creature attempted to snuggle under her chin. But suddenly she broke into a spate of coughing, deep and chesty. Struggled to breathe. Foo grabbed the mouse. 'Sorry, sorry. No good you excited too much.'

I hurried to fetch a nurse. We came running to find Kung Foo on his knees sobbing He was clutching Dervla's limp hand, her face serenely still, head lolling on the one side. I almost choked. The nurse stepped over and passed a hand over Dervla's eyes, closing them.

I hardly slept that night, tossing and turning, overwhelmed by regret that I wasn't there holding Dervla's hand when she passed. At that moment I swear I heard a single bell-like ring in the dark, lingering and drifting up the stairs from the lounge downstairs, almost as if it was seeking me out - a distinct sound I'd heard only once before.

I sat up startled, my heart pounding at a pace. I cast aside the bedcover, jumped up and tiptoed downstairs. The chalice sat still and innocent on the mantel piece, a gift from Dervla. I curled up on a couch and waited expectantly. Nothing. Was I simply mistaken? The sun was up when I awoke, having dozed off on the couch. I felt unusually rested and at peace.

Only much later I learned that the gift I'd received in gratitude from my dear departed friend wasn't a vessel to hold human remains, but a *Tibetan singing bowl* used in spiritual practice.

Arcobar Tales is now in print. An elegant little collection that, sadly, Dervla never got to see. It is dedicated to the magnificent staff of Nellie Melba Hospice. And that's where you may still pick up a copy – a gift to last a lifetime.

Afterword

Dr Siobhan Campbell, Open University UK, has researched and written about the place of creative and expressive writing in the communities involved in palliative care, supporting creativity and agency during some of the most important days of life.

The act of making something happen within language can increase the sick person's capacity to make sense of the randomness and seeming unfairness of life. Finding a voice with which to tell a story, whether one from our experience or one from our imagination, is an act of creation. In poetry, story and memoir, patients in palliative care, their friends, and those who have been bereaved can explore how creating an artwork in words can help to access the unsaid. Poetry and story can capture deep ambiguities through metaphor and symbol, acting as the opposite to dry medical jargon and instead expressing lived experience in personal and individual ways.

Acknowledgements

This short novella came together as a light-hearted diversion from my arduous task of attempting my first novel - which, I fear, may never be quite realised.

I wish to express my sincere appreciation to a gallant few who've read the novella in its early form and give me valuable feedback. These include my wife Neerosh, the playwright Kiren Carroll and a friendly neighbour who didn't wish to be named. Of course, I've had to count on Robert New to format the manuscript and turn it into a printed book that looks professional and presentable. Even so, *Arcobar Yarns* remains a work in progress. Further additions and changes may follow in due course.

About the Author

Bala Mudaly is an Indian South African, born in Durban in 1938. Chronic job insecurity and political harassment compelled him to migrate to Australia in 1988 with his wife.

He retired as a clinical psychologist from Monash Health in Melbourne in Dec 2018 at the age of 80.

His debut collection of poems and short stories set in Australia, *Colours of Hope and Despair*, was launched in 2018 and still available on Kindle. He has also had a short story, *Self-Inflected Pain of the Writer's Kind*, published in the Victorian Writer, a quarterly writers' magazine. The author has contributed short pieces to a fortnightly online publication of the University of KwaZulu Natal in Durban, the Creative Network Magazine. As an amateur writer, he has workshopped almost all his creative writings in a Writers Group sponsored by the City of Monash public library service. His memoir, Colour-Coated Identity, was his most ambitious creative non-fiction project published in 2021. He published a collection of musings, stories and non-fiction entitled *For All Seasons* in 2022.

Currently, the author is working on a novel with the tentative title: *Nothing's for Sure*. Its theme is the challenges of friendships and family relationships in post-apartheid South Africa beyond the constraints of race and colour.

Contact Bala at: bala.mudaly@gmail.com

Milton Keynes UK
Ingram Content Group UK Ltd.
UKHW022331161223
434454UK00009B/69